Mr. Bumba's
NEW
JOB

By Pearl Augusta Harwood
Pictures by Joseph Folger

Published by
Lerner Publications Company
Minneapolis, Minnesota

The type used
in this book is
MR. BUMBA TEXT
set in 16 point.

Library of Congress Catalog Card Number: 64-19774

Manufactured in the United States of America.
Published simultaneously in Canada by
The House of Grant, Toronto.

Second Printing 1964
Third Printing 1967
Fourth Printing 1968

Mr. Bumba lived in a big white house with green trim. On his fence Mr. Bumba had painted pictures of all sorts of things. It was the brightest fence in town.

Mr. Bumba was an artist. He liked to work in the back room of his house where the light was just right. But nowadays the back room was terribly noisy. Behind Mr. Bumba's backyard, men were building houses. They were building twenty-five new houses.

The new houses were behind Jane's backyard, too. That was next to Mr. Bumba's. They were also behind Bill's backyard, next to Mr. Bumba's on the other side. They were behind all the backyards on the street, where there had been a big orange grove.

Many orange trees had been cut down to make room for the new houses.

But the trees behind Mr. Bumba's yard had not all been cut down. Twenty-seven trees were left standing. They made a green belt behind his yard.

Jane's yard had a green belt behind it, too, and Bill's yard had one also.

Mr. Bumba was earning the money to buy
the whole green belt of orange trees. The land
cost a great deal. So Mr. Bumba had gone to
work for Mr. Perkins, who was building the new
houses.

Other men worked on the houses, too. The
houses grew quickly. Jane and Bill often watched
to see how fast the houses were being built.

Each house had a row of orange trees in front, a row of orange trees on each side, and a row of orange trees at the back of its lot. There was a small green belt around each new house.

Each house had a small patio. The patio was in back. It was like an outdoor living room.

Each patio had a fence around it on three sides. The house made the fourth side of the outdoor living room.

One Friday after school Jane and Bill went to look for Mr. Bumba. He was building fences in back of a new house.

"I think those fences look too much alike," said Jane.

"That is just what I was thinking," said Bill.

Mr. Bumba scratched his head. "I feel an idea coming," he said.

"Pictures!" shouted Jane. "Pictures on the patio fences!"

"How ever did you guess?" asked Mr. Bumba, smiling a wide smile.

"We will help you decide what the pictures will be about," said Jane.

"First we will have to ask Mr. Perkins," said Mr. Bumba.

"Can't you try one for him to see?" asked Bill.

"That will be just the thing," said Mr. Bumba. "I do not work on Saturdays. But I will come and do it tomorrow, just for fun. If Mr. Perkins does not like it, I can paint over the picture."

"We will come tomorrow and watch you," said Bill.

On Saturday morning they looked at the fences again.

"One picture, on one side of the patio, will be just right," Mr. Bumba said.

"On which side?" Jane asked.

"On the back side," said Bill. "Then you can see it when you look out of those big windows."

"I would like to see the ocean from my living room," said Jane.

"I would like to see a lake, and some deep, dark woods," said Bill.

"Very good ideas, both of them," said Mr. Bumba. "I think I can do <u>two</u> pictures for Mr. Perkins to see. One for this house, and one for the house next to this."

"Then you can try an ocean and a lake," said Jane happily.

"Will you do the lake first?" asked Bill.

"Well now, let me see," said Mr. Bumba, and scratched his head.

"Oh no," said Bill. "You should do the
ocean first, because that was the first idea."

So the first fence had an ocean painted on it. The second one had a lake, and some deep, dark woods.

After lunch, they all came back to see how the pictures looked. Mr. Perkins came around just then.

"What are you doing here on Saturday?" asked Mr. Perkins, looking at Mr. Bumba.

"I am just having some fun," said Mr. Bumba. "Jane and Bill have been giving me ideas."

Mr. Perkins went inside the living room. He looked out of the big windows that were really glass doors.

"Why, I can hardly believe it!" Mr. Perkins said. "The patio looks bigger and bigger. I am looking at the ocean way off there!"

They all went over to the next house. Mr. Perkins stood in that living room, and looked out of the big glass doors.

"Oh my, oh my!" said Mr. Perkins. "What a beautiful lake and woods."

"See the rowboat?" asked Bill.

"Yes, I want to jump right into it and start rowing," said Mr. Perkins.

"Do you think it would be a good idea to have a picture on each patio?" asked Mr. Bumba.

"I think it is a wonderful idea," said Mr. Perkins. "It is such a good idea, that I am going to have some other men build the fences, while you paint the pictures on them."

"I would like that very much," smiled Mr. Bumba. "Painting pictures is really fun for me."

"Can you make each picture different?" asked Mr. Perkins.

"Oh yes," said Mr. Bumba. "Jane and Bill will give me ideas every day."

"Wild animals in the jungle," said Bill.

"A mountain of snow with a ski lift," said Jane.

"Hold on!" said Mr. Perkins. "You must write the ideas down so you will not forget them. They all sound wonderful to me."

He pulled a pencil out of his pocket. He pulled out a little notebook, too. He tore some pages out of the notebook.

"You write them down," said Bill to Jane, and Jane began to write.

"I have another idea," said Mr. Bumba.

"Write it down!" said Jane and Bill, together.

"Some people who buy a house might have their own ideas for a picture," said Mr. Bumba.

"More kinds of boats," said Bill.

"Meadows with cows and horses," said Jane.

"If they do, I will send them to see you,"
Mr. Perkins said.

He walked up and down, whistling to himself.

"There will be no other place anywhere like
Green Belt Manor," said Mr. Perkins. "Everyone
will want to come here to live."

"More kinds of boats," said Bill.

"Meadows with cows and horses," said Jane.

"Hold on!" said Mr. Perkins. "You must write the ideas down so you will not forget them. They all sound wonderful to me."

He pulled a pencil out of his pocket. He pulled out a little notebook, too. He tore some pages out of the notebook.

"You write them down," said Bill to Jane, and Jane began to write.

"I have another idea," said Mr. Bumba.

"Write it down!" said Jane and Bill, together.

"Some people who buy a house might have their own ideas for a picture," said Mr. Bumba.

"Bumba's Village," said Jane softly to herself.

"Bumba's <u>Painted</u> Village," said Bill softly to himself.

"I think I am going to like my new job very much," said Mr. Bumba, out loud.

7271 1